PRINCE MARTIN
AND THE DRAGONS

PRINCE MARTIN

AND THE DRAGONS

BOOK THREE OF THE PRINCE MARTIN EPIC

BY BRANDON HALE

Illustrated by
JASON ZIMDARS

CONTENTS

PROLOGUE
A SHATTERED PEACE

The two daydreaming shepherds were watching their sheep. The flock quietly grazed; little lambs were asleep.

Mountain flowers were blooming bright yellow and blue, and the warm midday sun had dried up all the dew. Yearlings frolicked about, fully lost in their play. It seemed nothing could ruin that peaceful spring day.

Then two shadows were cast on the shepherds and sheep.

The shade that descended was sudden and deep.

The men got to their feet. Something wasn't quite right. The sheep began bleating and cowered in fright.

When the shepherds looked up, the words died on their lips: in the sky, they beheld a most dreadful eclipse! There were two silhouettes in the way of the sun. Something hovered above.

There was no time to run.

Then two screeches rang out in the valley that day.

The two terrible *dragons* had spotted their prey…

CHAPTER 1
RUMORS OF DRAGONS

In the meantime, just two hundred miles to the west, the King and his nobles and knights were distressed. There were rumors that dragons were spotted out east. And with each passing day, their concerns had increased.

Then a stranger showed up. He had fled from a place that two dragons destroyed. There was fear on his face. He described the two drakes to the King and his court, how they'd burned up his village—then killed just for sport. The man said the two dragons could never be slain for they spewed deadly fire like great torrents of rain. He said knights had fought back, but their shields would just melt in the face of the flames that those two dragons dealt.

When he'd learned all he could from his terrified guest, the King worried those wyrms would now visit The West.

(Those vile creatures were known by a number of terms, namely, *dragons* and *drakes* and, most dreadfully, *wyrms*.)

Now the mood in the castle got terribly tense, so the King called a council to plan their defense. From the castle, the carrier pigeons soon sped. They bore notes on their legs, and the messages read: "Rise in haste and come quickly for council of war; dragons approach—

at least two, maybe more!"

All the notes had been signed by the King of The West. They were stamped with his seal, and the notes were addressed to Protectors who lived in The West and beyond. Their duty was clear. Not one failed to respond.

In the following days, heroes heeded the call. They all came to the castle and met in the hall. The whole place was abuzz. Could the stories be true? There were warriors and knights and a wizard or two. And the King's stalwart Peers, with their glistening helms, stood by captains and kings from the neighboring realms.

And Prince Martin was there with his comrade, Sir Ray, a brave errant knight from a land far away.

Then SHE entered the room.

They all rose to their feet. They respectfully stood as *the Queen* took her seat.

She had golden-red hair and a beautiful face: a most elegant lady, abounding in grace. With a heart for the poor, she was caring and kind, and her beauty was matched by the strength of her mind.

Now the council began.

The King shared what he'd learned from the scared refugee whose poor village had burned. The King asked for advice, saying, "What should we do?"

From way off in the east, a foreboding wind blew.

The great hall now fell silent.

They pondered their fate.

The fire cast shadows.

The hour was late.

CHAPTER 2
THE WIZARD'S TALE

For a minute or more, no one stood up to speak. The whole situation seemed hopeless and bleak. They all knew about dragons; those fiends were a curse. They could sometimes be killed, but this duo seemed worse. Then a white-headed wizard stood up and he said:

> I can't help but recall an old book I once read. It was ages ago. I was eight (maybe nine). I'd been given a task by a tutor of mine for our Alchemy class, where we learned to make gold. It was just our first week when that schoolteacher told me to make a gold ring from two ounces of lead.
>
> I shyly asked, "How?"

"Look it up," she just said.

So I climbed down the stairs to the book vault below, where the wall torches flickered, a red-orange glow. Among ten thousand titles (quite possibly more), was a room that contained 'Metallurgical Lore.'

Now at this point, Prince Martin was feeling confused by a few of the words the old wizard had used. So the wizard, who once was a boy long before, kindly paused to explain "Metallurgical Lore." It involved mixing metals to make something new. What did "Alchemy" mean? Martin hadn't a clue! So the wizard explained that in ages of old they would take worthless lead and attempt to make *gold*. Thus, the wizard explained the strange terms to the Prince. Martin whispered his thanks for the words now made sense. Then the wizard continued the story he told of when *he* was a boy, long before he'd grown old:

My friends, as I was saying, a moment

before, a whole room had been marked 'Metallurgical Lore.'

In that room in the vault, I found row upon row filled with books about metals from ages ago.

I thought, *'A' is for Alchemy; that's where to start. There will surely be books on the gold-makers' art.* And I found one or two, which I set on the floor, yet continued to browse 'Metallurgical Lore.' Through the titles beginning with D, I had delved, till I came across one that I *thought* was miss-helved. On the spine, it said 'Drakes' in an old elven script.

And I shivered a bit in that scholarly crypt.

This is not about metals! I thought to myself, as I took the book down from its place on the shelf. I blew dust off the cover, revealing a pair of two crudely drawn dragons aloft in the air. When I opened the book, I could tell it was old: all the pages were yellowed and mottled with mold.

I sat down on the floor, and I started to read. And the tale was a spine-chilling saga, indeed! I looked up, and I thought, *Can this story be true?* I continued to read. My uneasiness grew.

And I sat there for hours, absorbed in the tale. When I finished that book, I was frightened and pale.

The book told of two dragons, both grim and both grave. Every *two thousand years*, they'd emerge from their cave. There was one that was black, and the other was red. And the book made it clear the two fiends were well fed.

They breathed in the cold air, but blew out deadly flames. Mortis and Ardoris, those were their names. I would translate them roughly to 'Death' and to 'Fire.'

To destroy all mankind was the villains' desire.

They had teeth sharp as daggers, all jagged and white. They had talons for shredding, as black as the night. They had terrible wings and could speed through the air. The mere sound of their screeches made armies despair.

They would wake for one year; then those wyrms would repair to another location to make a new lair. They would search for a cave or a hole in the ground, one so dark and remote that they couldn't be found. They would fall back to sleep—a two-thousand-year rest—in the depths of that desolate, pestilent nest.

Oh, but woe to mankind when the wyrms were awake, which those living would label 'The Year of the Drake'! They'd emerge even worse when each cycle began, increasingly reckless and fearing no man.

They'd lay waste to whole cities; just rubble remained. They could not be shot down, much less captured or chained. They would level a village; and, when they were done, they would eat until full and then kill just for fun.

It seemed humans were cursed, for those drakes never died. They'd not even been wounded, though many had tried. Mighty warriors had challenged those arrogant drakes, tried to seize an advantage, exploit their mistakes. But the shields that they carried would *melt in the heat* the two dragons produced. Many died in defeat.

That sad cycle existed for time out of mind. No one quite understood why they hated mankind.

When I read that old book, I was merely a boy. And believe me, my friends, that it gives me no joy to retell such a tale on a dark, stormy night. And I urgently hope that my theory's not right!

But the rumors that reach us from lands to the east have convinced me *those dragons have come out to feast...*

Then they all spoke at once. A cold fear gripped the hall, but the King raised a hand, and it silenced them all.

They turned back to the wizard. (They thought they were doomed.) The King said, "Continue." The wizard resumed:

But be bold and take heart, O you men of The West! For our fate isn't sealed. There is *more* to be stressed. In the back of that book had been added a note (an appendix of sorts) where a scrivener wrote of a long-distant past when the wyrms were awake, leaving smoldering ruins and death in their wake.

And atop a tall mountain there lived a rare breed of small elves who attempted a great-hearted deed. *They'd endeavored to forge both a shield and a spear to destroy the two drakes by the end of that year.*

The great shield was the key. 'Twas the first of their aims: one to shelter a hero from fiery flames.

A sharp spear would come next, one to pierce dragon hearts.

They'd discovered advanced metallurgical arts!

They'd been swinging their picks when they happened to find a unique strain of silver in tunnels they mined. They extracted the lode and returned to their cave. Those diminutive miners then eagerly gave what they'd found to their blacksmiths, whose forges were fanned. Soon the silver lode glowed like a fiery brand.

Having melted the silver, they mixed some with steel, and the red molten metals began to congeal. All the blacksmiths then gathered, observing at length, that the alloy they'd made had *incredible strength*. They confirmed their conclusion by running a test to observe how the alloy reacted when stressed.

They first held it to flames—yet the alloy stayed cool. Then they fanned their great forge, and they heaped on the fuel. The forge burned like the sun, and it roared like a gale. Then they tossed in the alloy and didn't exhale for a minute, it seemed; then they pulled it back out—still cool to the touch!

That removed the last doubt.

Then a blacksmith's apprentice spoke up, and he said that the strangest idea had entered his head. The youth stammered a bit with excitement and zeal while suggesting a use for the silvery steel. He first drew them some sketches (admittedly rough). Then he measured the silver: just barely enough. As the youth kept on talking, it soon became plain: *they could forge two great weapons to have the drakes slain!*

Then it hit them at once: they must try to conceal their intent to make weapons from silver and steel! For the elves were not foolish; they rightly assumed that if word got around, then their work would be doomed. For the dragons would come and destroy their designs (not to mention their foundries and forges and mines).

They debated all night, and then plans coalesced: they'd send word to the king of a land south and west. They had heard of his legend through story and song: he was said to be big and courageous and strong. The elves used their lone pigeon to send him a note. (Their words were encoded, but here's what they wrote.)

They described the new alloy of silver and steel. He must take it on trust that the marvel was real. They next told of their plans for a spear and a shield, which that man among men could effectively wield. They would first forge the shield to resist sudden heat—so that king would not ever be forced to retreat. They would next make the spear with the greatest of care, so it aerodynamically flew through the air. Thus, the shield could first block a drake's fiery breath. Such a silvery spear could then deal the thing death!

That lone message the blacksmiths dispatched to that king said they'd make every effort to finish by spring. The elves vowed not to rest till the weapons were made—ever living in fear the two dragons would raid. They would give them as gifts for humanity's sake, to at last put an end to the Year of the Drake.

So that king and his court had to patiently wait for the elves and the shield and the spear and their fate.

A cold winter arrived.

And then spring came and went.

But those elves never came, so a rider was sent to their mountain to see if the weapons were made. But he never rode back. That king now was afraid. He prepared for the worst. His realm waited in fear. Then the skies up above grew pacific and clear! Watchmen scanned the blue skies, but no drake could be seen. And they wondered about what this portent could mean. A whole month came and went. Had the two dragons gone? Soon the peace was restored, and hope rose like the dawn.

But the elves and their work were not heard from again. And their memory faded in kingdoms of men. They were lost to the past, ancient history's fog.

I've thus told you the tale of that strange epilogue. And Alas! I don't know where those things all occurred, for the old script was faded and lines had been blurred. I did get the impression the weapons were made, but were never delivered—forever delayed.

Now those wyrms are awake. My heart tells me it's so. We must make preparations to strike a hard blow. Let us search for those weapons to which our hopes cling!

When the old wizard finished, they turned to the King. He looked grim and determined, a pillar of strength. He consulted the Queen, and they whispered at length.

Then he sat there in silence.

He furrowed his brow, then declared, "The man's right. We must find them somehow! Go and search for those weapons and bring them to me. And then *I'll* fight the dragons. You've heard my decree."

The King sent the Protectors to search two by two.

And to Martin and Ray, he said, "*You're* needed too. Go and gather your friends. Form your brotherly band. We need your assistance to scour the land. We must locate that shield and that silvery spear. The dark is descending; we must persevere. In the darkest of hours, hope always ascends."

So Prince Martin and Ray would go gather their friends. They would leave right away, the next morning at dawn. They'd enlist their two friends, Theodosius and John.

CHAPTER 3
THE QUEST BEGINS

And so Martin the Prince and the knight named Sir Ray took a trip to the forest. They dared not delay.

They'd first met in that wood when a dangerous pack of wild hogs had decided to mount an attack on an innocent fawn. The fawn's peril was great. It was then by pure chance, through a strange twist of fate, that Sir Ray wandered by and he heard the fawn's plight. *And Sir Ray was no cur who would shy from a fight.* The dog rushed to its aid and protected the deer. Then Prince Martin showed up—and though stricken with fear—the boy entered the ruckus and fought beside Ray. They defeated those hogs on that crisp autumn day. But Sir Ray had been hurt, badly

bitten and gored. Martin carried him home—
and he won his first sword! Now a friendship
had formed between Martin and Ray that was
stronger than steel and would not fade away.

They remembered that day, as they raced
to the tree that was home to the elf that they
needed to see. They soon found Theodosius,
who lent them his ear. Martin told of the drakes
and the shield and the spear. And this wood elf,
who went by the shorter name, "Ted," knew a
great many things and was very well read. As
a Treetender elf, Ted ensured all the trees were
well cared for and pruned and kept free of dis-
ease. And this Treetender also did all that he
could to protect the small creatures who lived
in the wood. He was handy with rope from his
time in the trees; he could rope and rappel with
the greatest of ease. As they sat in his treehouse
atop a great oak, the elf listened intently as
Prince Martin spoke.

The elf Ted was disturbed by the Prince's
report; but with no hesitation, he pledged his
support. He took down an old book, which he

read for a while. The elf nodded his head, and he said with a smile, "Now I think that I know where those weapons were made. The realm will sure need them when dragons invade. We must climb to the top of a mountain most high, to a cave that's remote, hidden up in the sky. If I'm right, we'll discover that spear and that shield to bring back to the King for his strong arms to wield.

"But that mountain is far, to the north and the east: a one hundred and twenty-mile journey, at least. The two dragons are coming. We must travel fast. But how can we cover a distance that vast?"

"I have got an idea," the boy told the elf. And he secretly smiled as he thought to himself of a fellow they knew who would jump at the chance to help them all cross that enormous expanse.

"I'll explain in a bit what it is I've got planned. But first, let's get John. We must round out our band."

So they ran to the lair of a timberwolf pack— which I don't recommend because wolves can attack. Oh, but *these* wolves were friendly,

especially John, who was known for his brains just as much as his brawn. With his keen ears and sight, John the wolf was quite wild, but stayed calm and collected—unless he was riled. They'd met John in the forest when he was ensnared. Things were scary at first, and his fangs had been bared. But the boy and the dog helped the wolf to escape. Then John paid them both back when they'd got in a scrape. John was now their companion, a friend to the end—the kind who was eager to guard and defend.

They told John the whole story of silver and steel. The wolf didn't once doubt the two dragons were real. "Count on me," John declared, "to do all that it takes to support the King's efforts to kill those two drakes."

So the elf and the wolf and the dog and the lad would begin a great quest, and it made their hearts glad. It was quite a reunion. Our friends were all smiles.

Then the Prince shared his plan for traversing the miles. "We should first go to town. We'll go see our old friend. He'll be happy to see us and eager to lend us a hand, for he owes us a favor or two. We'll just pop in and visit, right out of the blue."

They all grinned when they heard what the boy had in mind. For their lives and this fellow's were now intertwined. As they walked, our four friends couldn't help but recall an adventure they'd had in the previous fall. It had brought

them together and formed their brave band;
they now did daring deeds all across the King's
land!

CHAPTER 4
AN OLD FRIEND

They arrived at an inn on the main street of town. Martin entered and asked if his friend was around.

"I just heard him roll in. He's been out for a ride. He's out back in the stable," the owner replied.

When they saw their old friend, they could not help but grin. It was sure good to see the old fellow again!

He was tuning his coach, and he didn't look up, unlike his companion, a little brown pup. The hound yapped and she yapped, a small bundle of fur. The man lowered his wrench and looked over at her. Then he noticed our friends, and he said with a grin, "It's all right, Virginia; we'll let them come in."

Then he scooped up the pup, who suspiciously eyed our four friends. They just smiled and proceeded inside.

That was how they found *Tim*, with his workbench and tools and his secondhand coach and his oat-munching mules!

Though he walked with a stoop, Tim was hearty and hale. He now worked as a coachman who carried the mail. They had met the old fellow the previous fall in a story of thieves they'd forever recall. Old Tim's life had been changed in the ninety days since he'd first tramped into town—and encountered the Prince.

They asked Tim for a ride.

"Hop on board!" he replied.

So the four daring heroes climbed up and inside.

The man harnessed the mules, scooped the pup off the ground, and they sat side by side, both old Tim and the hound.

With a crack of the reins, Tim's coach shot from the gate, and they raced down the highway. The coach headed straight for that northeastern

mountain the elf had in mind. They would search through its cave on their mission to find those two marvelous weapons—that shield and that spear—so the realm would be ready if drakes should appear.

CHAPTER 5
AN ENCOUNTER WITH THE QUEEN

When the coach had arrived at the outskirts of town, Martin saw the Queen's carriage. Her driver slowed down.

She stepped out of the coach, which was blocking the lane. The Queen smiled at her son, as she held a gold chain. *And attached to the chain was a lock of her hair*, which was fixed by a hairpin with feminine care. It was *then* that the sun pierced a path through the haze, and that lock of hair glimmered in those golden rays.

The Queen greeted the Prince with a kiss on the cheek. "Son, I hope you discover those weapons you seek. The whole realm is depending on heroes like you. Don't you ever give up, son, whatever you do."

Then she lifted the chain, and the boy bowed his head. As she hung it around Martin's neck, the Queen said, "Wear this close to your heart in remembrance of me. Sometimes danger and darkness are all we can see. If you're stricken by fear and can no longer cope, then remember my love—and do *not* give up hope."

The Queen tucked it beneath the boy's shirt nice and snug. Then she gave him a smile and a very big hug.

She thanked Tim for his help. He could not meet her eye. He just blushed and looked down. (Tim was terribly shy.)

Then she whispered to John and to Ted and to Ray: "Keep an eye on my boy." Then the Queen rode away. She returned to the castle, the royal abode.

And our friends' quest continued; Tim raced down the road. They saw hamlets and fields and small farms rolling by. They would help save The West. Or at least they would try. Though

The West was worth saving from dragons and fire, our friends couldn't have guessed what the feat would require.

CHAPTER 6
THE WYRMS MAKE THEIR WAY WEST

The wyrms spotted a village! They beat their great wings. To burn houses was one of their favorite things.

They brought murder and mayhem wherever they went. Now like two shooting stars, they began their descent.

They'd bring death to this village. Their wicked hearts thrilled. And they boastfully thought, *We can never be killed.*

And as Mortis and Ardoris made their approach, the drakes burst through a cloud bank and spotted a coach. It left town in a hurry. It raced down the lane.

Then an evil thought entered old Mortis's brain.

The drake flew to the coach, which it seized in its claws. Mortis carried it up to the red drake's applause.

Mortis let the coach drop.

The coach fell back to earth. And the wicked old hearts of the drakes filled with mirth.

Then the dragons both landed and stood there beside the sad wreck of the coach. And three people inside—

After eating, one said, "We should visit The West. But first, let's return to our cave to digest. We will rest a few days; then with *terrible force*, we'll bring death to The West."

They felt zero remorse.

Meanwhile, ninety miles west, Tim was making good time. His coach raced down the road, which had started to climb; for the altitude slowly but surely increased as they made their way north and then curved to the east.

When they'd traveled two days at a very brisk pace, they could see in the distance a mountain's broad base.

"There it is," said the elf. "I don't like it a bit.

I had hoped it was smaller, I'll freely admit."

The road ended abruptly—they couldn't tell why—a few miles from the mountain that loomed in the sky. The great highways were old (about two thousand years). They'd been built for exploring these northern frontiers. But they hadn't been finished—not this one, at least. All the work done on this one had suddenly ceased.

They thanked Tim for the ride. He would wait down below. The terrain was too rough for his carriage to go.

As they hiked toward the mountain, the thing seemed to grow. It was dotted with pines and white patches of snow. They saw water cascading from spigots on high. Towards the top, the tall mountain was scraping the sky.

It was shrouded in mist. Lightning pulsed at the peak. It was dark and forbidding. Our friends didn't speak. The mountain looked deadly, so full of unknowns. Up above, thunder rumbled; it rattled their bones.

They had food for their journey and flint for a fire and a tent for a rest when their bodies would tire. The young Prince had his sword. Ted had plenty of rope. But the boy felt a shortage of courage and hope. After checking their gear, they got ready to climb. There was no time to lose in this race against time. They assumed the two drakes were out flying around. Oh, somehow that shield and that spear must be found!

But the mountain before them was hard to behold; it looked rocky and rugged and cruel and cold.

CHAPTER 7
THE MURDEROUS MOUNTAIN

The four friends all stared up at the mountain with dread. They did not have high hopes for the journey ahead.

When he saw what great fear that tall mountain produced, it was clear to Sir Ray his friends needed a boost. He encouraged his comrades: "We can't give up now! We've made it this far. We should all take a vow to refuse to give up and to never say 'quit.' We must call up our courage, resilience, and grit."

So they all took a vow to do all that they could. They would scale that tall mountain, and when they all stood at its peak, they would rest and then search for the cave. They drew strength

from the thought of the lives they might save.

So they climbed up the mountain's sharp, steady incline, way up into mist, where the sun didn't shine. The bad weather got worse; the sky started to sleet, and the path grew quite slippery under their feet. The wind howled in their ears; it was all they could hear. If one slipped and he fell, he might well disappear! Our friends dared not look down. What a terrible drop! But they climbed, and they climbed, till they got to the top.

They saw boulders and pines and a deep, misty lake. At the edge of a cliff, they sat down for a break. For a moment the sun pierced a path through the gloom. And The West, which they loved—where the wildflowers bloom—could just barely be seen from the mountain's great height. The sight filled them with hope, like a beacon at night.

As they rested, John said that he thought he could see the dark mouth of a cave by an ever-green tree.

Ted announced that the cave must be fully

explored: he was sure it was where those old weapons were stored!

So they went to that cavern, a five-minutes' walk. It was carved in the granite, the wind-blasted rock.

After walking inside, the thought crossed Martin's mind: he'd forgotten his sword, which he *had* to go find! For that sword was the finest thing Martin possessed. He had oiled down the blade when they'd stopped for that rest. After John spied the cave, they had been in a rush. Now his absence of mind made the young fellow blush. Martin felt like a fool for forgetting his blade. He did not tell his friends of this blunder he'd made.

He ran back to the ledge where they'd stopped for that rest—that high rocky cliff with a view of The West. Martin looked for his sword, which he easily found by a rock where he'd left it, right there on the ground.

As he stood on the ledge, he was hoping to see one last glimpse of his home and the great Western Sea. But the mist had returned and obstructed his view. Now the sky up above had an ominous hue. The boy felt a hot wind from the north and the east. The wind blew up behind him—then suddenly ceased...

CHAPTER 8
THE CLASH ON THE CLIFF

All at once, the ground trembled beneath the boy's feet, as the back of his neck felt a gust of damp heat. A horrible stench was assaulting his nose.

The boy shivered with fright from his head to his toes. All his hairs stood on end. His skin started to crawl. Martin thought he might faint. He felt helpless and small.

There was something behind him.

He felt its hot breath.

He instinctively sensed the close presence of death.

He did not want to look. Was it all a bad dream? But he turned and he stared and he started to scream.

Martin's cry traveled far through that thin mountain air.

It sounded of terror and utter despair: for a dragon had landed and lurked by the boy, whom it hated at once—whom it longed to destroy!

With a hideous leer, the black dragon declared, "Boy, you look a bit pale, but you mustn't be scared. Would you like to sit down? I don't want you to swoon. Would you join me for lunch? It is nearly high noon. Oh, I *do* love a picnic—but *what* shall we eat? I don't know about you...but I'm partial to meat!"

Then the black dragon giggled; poor Martin felt sick. The drake was now drooling, so oily and slick.

"Boy, I hope you'll forgive me. I *do* love my jests. But you must understand, it's so rare we have guests."

As it grinned, the boy saw the drake's terrible teeth.

Martin secretly lowered a hand to his sheath.

The boy fingered the hilt of his sharp little sword. He well knew the black dragon would quickly get bored with its comments and quips.

His life hung by a thread.

Then the dragon stopped grinning and soberly said, "I will eat you, of course. Oh, but first you will burn! I *do* hope your kind will eventually learn that to meddle with dragons is very unwise."

The drake giggled again—but had death in its eyes.

Martin knew he would soon be enveloped in flame. So he yanked out his sword—and with no time to aim—the boy hurled the bright blade, and it struck with its point!

And the blade buried deep in the dragon's wing joint!

The blade hit where the fiend lost a few of its scales, which cover such wyrms from their heads to their tails. The beast bellowed in rage at the gall of the lad. With a wing badly wounded, that dragon was mad!

But the boy was now swordless—no means of defense. The black dragon came closer and hissed at the Prince.

There was nowhere to run. What a horrible bind! The wyrm was in front; an abyss was behind.

The drake's nostrils expanded, inhaling the air. The boy thought he was finished.

He'd die, then and there.

It appeared that the tales of Prince Martin were through—he'd be burned to a crisp when flames started to spew.

Then a white streak of fury burst in on the scene!

It ferociously roared like a crazed wolverine. With a wrath rarely seen in the long ages since, *the white knight* stood between the black drake and the Prince!

The dog's lips were curled back; Sir Ray's fangs were revealed. He protected his Prince like a powerful shield.

With a rage in his eye that came deep from within, the dog growled at the drake, "Let the battle begin!"

And the wyrm was surprised when the white knight attacked! It all happened so fast; the drake couldn't react: Sir Ray crouched and he sprang and he flew through the air—right before the first blazes had started to flare.

Having leaped on its neck, the dog seized the drake's ear!

Ray had razor-sharp teeth. Now pain started

to sear through the ear of the dragon, now thoroughly crazed. It blew blankets of flame. It was no longer fazed!

The black drake whipped its neck and attempted to throw the white dog off the cliff—but Ray wouldn't let go. The drake reared up and twisted. It arched and it bucked.

The poor Prince scrambled back, and he dodged and he ducked all the fiery blasts bursting forth from the beast.

But the dog held on tight.

The drake's madness increased. And its powerful feet were now pounding the ground, and it *cracked* from the weight of the wyrm and the hound!

The boy screamed, "Let it go, Ray, the cliff's going to break!"

But the knight held on tight to the ear of the drake.

With the dragon still thrashing and spewing its fire, the plight of the dog was exceedingly dire.

"Get back now!" growled the dog to the

boy through his teeth. Sir Ray managed to add, "Don't get caught underneath!"

So the youngster sprang back.

It was *then* the cliff broke.

The two enemies fell in a curtain of smoke!

Martin watched from above as the drake and the dog hurtled down into space, disappearing in fog. An eternity passed, till a far distant sound told the boy the big dragon had crashed to the ground. Martin shouted Ray's name, and he bitterly cried.

But only the howl of a whirlwind replied.

Then the wolf and the elf both arrived at his side. They were panting for breath.

And the three of them cried.

Left to grieve were the boy, Theodosius, and John.

They thought Ray had been lost.

They were sure he was gone.

CHAPTER 9
THE QUEST CONTINUES

Martin finally told his two friends, John and Ted: "'We must finish our quest'—that's what Ray would have said."

So, despondent, they entered the cave John had found. In its depths, they discovered a frightening mound. 'Twas a pile of bleached bones. They were not big at all. Like the elves of the mountains, the bones were quite small. Ted declared, "These are old—about two thousand years. I did not expect *this*, which exceeds my worst fears."

And surrounding the bones was a sad disarray of what once was a workshop, now left to decay. All the tools had been scattered, great forges destroyed.

For this once was a place where small elves were employed!

Then the clash on the cliff flashed in Prince Martin's head. He tried hard to recall what that dragon had said. Then it suddenly struck him: that wyrm had said *"we"* when it spoke about guests and it giggled with glee. They had thought the two dragons were bound for The West. But what if they'd gone to their cave for a rest? He knew one of the dragons—*the black one*—was dead. Oh! But where was the other—the one that was *red*?

Then it dawned on the boy: this cave *now* was a lair!

Should they search for the spear and the shield? Did they dare?

Martin told his two friends, who did not like this news. *But bravery's not natural; it's something we choose.*

And though frightened, they searched through the cave, dank and dark. They *must* find those weapons so they could embark on their long journey back, to their homes in The West.

Then the timberwolf whispered, "I've spotted a chest."

Our friends ran to the chest and were thoroughly shocked: it was just the right size.

But the chest had been locked!

So they searched for the key, leaving no stone unturned. Oh, what would they do if a dragon returned?

Then John suddenly stopped, and he stood there inert.

His hackles shot up, and his ears were alert.

All at once, they could feel the ground tremor and quake. Had something just landed? They felt their knees shake. A dark shape then appeared at the mouth of the cave. Now our friends' situation was terribly grave.

The shape entered the cave.

They heard scales scrape on stone.

It was clear our three friends were no longer alone!

Then they heard a voice echo throughout the dark dome, a hideous voice that said, "*Mortis,*

I'm home. I've been out for a swim. Now there's work to be done. We'll rain fire on The West. This is sure to be fun!"

The thing giggled a bit as it moved through the cave.

And not one of our friends felt the slightest bit brave.

As it slowly approached, they could see it was red, with sharp spikes on its back and great horns on its head. Our friends looked at each other, their eyes open wide.

Should they run or attack or find someplace to hide?

The wolf whispered to Martin, "You search for the key."

Then John turned to the elf, and the two did agree: they'd distract the red dragon to buy the boy time. From the depths of the cave, the two started their climb.

When they reached the main cavern, the wyrm was inside. So they stepped into view and quite loudly they cried, "Hey, you dimwitted wyrm!" Then they raced from the cave.

And the red dragon chased them; their blood it did crave!

The beast followed them both to the light of the day, as it blew flaming blasts at the backs of its prey.

Then it burst from the cave and confronted the pair.

The drake snarled as it said, "You two picked the wrong lair! All who dare to intrude in our cavern must die." With a hiss, it declared, "You two fools will now fry!"

But the wolf, with a lunge, bit the beast on its tail—just as Ted threw his lasso and watched the loop sail through the air till it caught 'round

the red dragon's neck! It blew fire at the elf, but the elf hit the deck.

Having dodged that great blast, the elf rushed to the pine; and around its thick trunk, the elf wrapped his long line. Ted had tethered the beast to the mountain's tall peak! But our friends' situation was still very bleak. For the tree, although made of the stoutest of stuff, couldn't stand the drake's strength; it was *not* strong enough.

As our friends hid by boulders, just south of the tree, they gaped as the drake tried to rip itself free.

Its broad wings beat the air, and up rose the big brute. With tremendous hard tugs, the drake strained at each root. There was cracking and popping, and chunks of dirt flew as the roots burst asunder; the tree leaned askew.

The red dragon had nearly uprooted the pine! Our friends looked to the cave, and they longed for a sign that the boy had discovered the shield and the spear.

They needed help *now*.

Would Prince Martin appear?

CHAPTER 10
A LIGHT SHINES IN THE DARKNESS

While all this had transpired, the young Prince had to look for the key to the chest in each cranny and nook of that desolate cavern, so dark and so dank. There were spiders—and worse—and that dragons' lair stank.

The boy desperately searched but could not find the key! He'd left no stone unturned. He cried, "Where can it be?"

His friends needed his help. There were tears in his eyes. Then he looked toward the entrance and got a surprise.

Through the cave's open mouth, the sun cast a lone beam.

It caused something to sparkle, a faint little gleam!

Martin looked at his chest, saw the Queen's lock of hair.

And it shimmered a bit in that shadowy lair.

It now hung from his shirt, which his mother had sewn—for the chain had slipped out when he'd lifted a stone. And the hair was attached by a small golden pin.

…It was three inches long…

…It was straight…

…It was thin…

The boy grabbed the gold hairpin! He suddenly knew what it was that the pin might allow him to do.

Martin raced to the chest and inserted the pin.

He could feel the mechanical pieces within.

The boy jiggled the pin and attempted to pick the brass lock of the chest.

Then he heard something click.

The lock opened at last! Martin lifted the lid. Then he looked in the chest to see what the thing hid.

The boy sighed with relief.

He found resting inside *the great shield and the spear that could pierce a drake's hide*!

How they glimmered and gleamed! What a wonderful sight. They were cool to the touch and amazingly light.

The boy quickly assembled the shield and the spear.

He remembered Sir Ray.

He no longer felt fear.

CHAPTER 11
MARTIN THE AVENGER

Martin raced to his friends, who now needed his aid.

And this is the stuff of which legends are made!

With the shield on his arm and the spear in his hand, the young boy took a breath then the *Prince* took his stand! Martin surged from the cave with the courage he'd found—just as the drake ripped the tree from the ground.

With a glance at the tree, the drake burned it to ash with a burst of its breath, in a fiery flash. The fiend did it for show, to exhibit its might and to fill its next victims with terror and fright. For a moment the dragon admired the effects. Then to John and to Ted, it said, *"You're* burning next!"

As it beat its broad wings, looming over the two, the brave boy, with a battle cry, charged into view!

The beast turned its attention from John and from Ted to the boy with a look that said, *Blood will be shed.*

Then it noticed the shield and the silvery spear.

For the first time in ages, that drake tasted fear!

And then Ardoris blew flaming blasts at the boy, whom it hoped to burn badly, to fully destroy.

But the Prince stood his ground with his shield held up high.

He repulsed the drake's fire that rained down from the sky.

And the shield kept its cool!

The drake sucked in more air, ever eying the Prince with a horrified stare.

Then the elf and the timberwolf heard Martin say, just under his breath, "I'll do *this* for Sir Ray!"

Martin reared back his arm—and he let the spear fly.

Like a comet it flashed as it flew through the sky!

The drake twisted in terror to dodge the boy's dart.

But the silver tip struck—and it plunged through the heart!

A loud shriek then escaped from the mouth of the beast.

The drake's beating wings slowed then they suddenly ceased.

Then the dead dragon plummeted end over end.

And it hit the ground hard, never more to ascend!

It was there that it lay, in a smoldering heap— no more to raze towns or attack helpless sheep.

Thus, the mountain elves' sacrifice *wasn't* in vain! It took two thousand years, but it ended the reign of the terrible dragons that prowled the earth. Those elves died never knowing their offering's worth…

CHAPTER 12
THE SURPRISE OF THEIR LIVES

With the red dragon's death, the bright sun showed its face. As it burned off the mist, our friends went to the place where Sir Ray had been lost, that most terrible ledge. And with tears in their eyes, they approached its sharp edge.

Since the clouds and the mist had by now disappeared, our friends stood at the edge of the cliff and they peered at the dark speck below where the black dragon lay. They lamented the loss of the knight named Sir Ray.

Then a small patch of white caught the timber-wolf's eye.

The wolf studied it hard, and he couldn't

deny that it looked like *a dog*. Was it held there in space by *a bush* jutting out from that sheer rocky face?

Then John shouted with joy, for Sir Ray was alive!

That bush had arrested his long downward dive!

The white knight shouted out as he hung down below.

And Ted was sure glad he had lanyards in tow! He uncoiled a long rope with a loop at the end. He would let it out fast; he would *lasso* his friend.

Sir Ray shouted, "The roots are beginning to rip, and I'd rather not finish this long downward trip!"

Then in silence, the wolf and the boy watched in awe, as Ted lowered the rope—and he caught the dog's paw!

The bush fell into space.

But the canine did not!

He was dangling there. He had safely been caught!

Then all three gripped the rope, and they started to haul the dog up from the depths; they would *not* let him fall!

When they'd raised him back up, Ray was broiled and scraped. As they hugged him, they asked him how he had escaped.

"As we fell, I could tell that the fiend couldn't fly. And I had to do something; at least I must try. I released the drake's ear, and I gave a hard push. I flew off of the fiend, and I crashed in that bush.

"I was stunned, and its screeches still rang in my ear. If you had been calling, well, I couldn't hear. And my jaw cramped up tightly; I couldn't call out to announce I'd got loose and was free of that lout. I hung in there and thought quite a bit of you three. And I didn't once doubt you'd come looking for me."

Then they went to the place where the red dragon lay. "I'm pretty impressed!" said the knight named Sir Ray.

Then the elf cut a claw from the drake's scaly foot, where it lay in the ashes and smoldering soot, and the Prince pulled the spear from the beast's scaly breast. To be sure, they had more than completed their quest!

"I'll admit I've been dreading our long journey back," said the Prince, with a sigh, as he shouldered his pack.

Ted replied, "Then there's something you really must see." The elf turned to the cave and said, "Come follow me! My book mentioned a secret way out of the cave, which the mountain elves took for the time it could save. As we searched for the key, I discovered *a boat*. I sure hope the thing's sturdy; we'll need it to float."

And the boy and the dog and the wolf were confused.

But the elf was insistent; he'd not be refused.

They returned to the cave. They all followed the elf, who couldn't help smiling in spite of himself.

They went deep in the cave, yet the light seemed to grow. And still deeper they delved till they saw a green *glow*.

In amazement, the Prince asked what caused the green light.

"They're *glowworms*!" cried Ted, with a grin of delight.

CHAPTER 13
THE WILDEST RIDE

In the depths of the cave was the loveliest glow, which illumined the work of the elves long ago. Tiny worms were attached to the ceiling and walls, and they lit up stalactites, a river, and falls.

The elf showed them the boat which now sat on the shore. It had benches for sitting, but only one oar. And the river flowed *fast*; this was no gentle stream.

It was then John declared, "I do *not* like this scheme. But I'd rather not walk." The exhausted wolf sighed. "So for better or worse, I'm along for the ride."

Martin asked Ted to steer. The elf picked up the oar. And they worried a bit about what was in store. Our friends boarded the boat, which they launched from the bank, and the swift current pulled them away with a yank. Then the brotherly band had a rollicking ride down the cavern's cold river; they rode its swift tide!

As they shot rushing rapids, great boulders appeared. Ted avoided them all as he skillfully steered. On this breathtaking ride, they all kept their teeth clenched; but they'd whoop and they'd laugh every time they got drenched!

After riding an hour, Ted spotted a light. The elf shouted, "A *waterfall*! Time to hold tight!"

Soon they heard a huge waterfall roaring ahead. The wolf muttered, "I wish we were walking instead." Then the craft turned a corner. They squinted their eyes as the sunlight burst in. "This is *really* not wise!" shouted John as they raced toward that deafening roar. He said, "Ted, please assure me you've done this before!"

The elf shook his head no with a hesitant look. "But the mountain elves did it, or so said my book!"

They shot forth from a spout by the mountain's wide base! And they all held their breath as they dropped into space. With a marvelous splash, the boat landed below, where the whitewater rapids continued to flow.

"That worked out pretty well!" said the elf with a grin.

"Nicely done," said the wolf. "Never do that again."

When they passed the sharp rocks where the black dragon struck, Martin leaned from the boat and his sword he did pluck from old Mortis's wing. The boy washed off the blade. (The sword was unharmed; it was wonderfully made.)

In the distance, they saw the old cobblestone road. And the river meandered, it snaked, and it flowed to the highway where Tim and Virginia the hound had been patiently waiting below on the ground.

Tim had stew in the pot and a crackling fire. The companions warmed up and they got a bit drier.

Ted told Tim the whole story. Tim listened in awe. Then Ted showed him the proof: the red dragon's black claw! Then they showed Tim the corpse of the nasty black drake. Now the coach-man knew why he had felt the earth shake! Tim then told them he'd seen bright explosions of light that had flashed through the mist from the mountain's great height. Tim declared he'd heard screeches that came from on high. He'd been terribly worried the dragons were nigh!

Then the Prince had another big favor to ask. He said, "Tim, would you mind doing one final task? Would you drive to the castle and kindly explain that the weapons are found—and the drakes have been slain? Please inform them we're safe, and there's nothing to fear; they can call off the quest for the shield and the spear. Say the cycle's been broken; allay all their fears of those drakes coming now—or in two thousand years. Take this talon as proof. They will see and believe that the dragons are dead; this is no mere reprieve.

"As for us, we'll return by this boat we've obtained. We'll be two days behind you," Prince

Martin explained. "This river will bear us. We'll lazily rest, enjoying the scenes as we float to The West."

So old Tim rode ahead. As he spread the good news, our four friends all relaxed on their riverboat cruise. As they floated southwest, they saw beautiful scenes. It was springtime, of course, and you know what that means: all the flowers were blooming. The robins were out. The crops in the fields were beginning to sprout.

When they reached the King's realm, they were greeted with cheers, and the songs of their bravery were sung through the years. But what Martin would always remember the best was the clash on the cliff when Sir Ray passed the test.

'Twas the test of true friendship.

It's easy to fail.

When we're scared and uncertain, our hearts feel so frail.

But Ray proved that in danger and peril and strife, for his friend, whom he loved, he would lay down his life.

THE END

Coming soon

Prince Martin and the Cave Bear!

Visit *www.princemartin.com* to download the prologue and first chapter. It's completely free!

. . .

More Prince Martin

If you enjoyed *Prince Martin and the Dragons*, you won't want to miss Books 1 and 2 of the Prince Martin Epic: *Prince Martin Wins His Sword* and *Prince Martin and the Thieves*! Find them at: *www.princemartin.com*

ABOUT THE AUTHOR

When Brandon Hale was a young boy, he lived in South America. It was a great place to be a kid, and his mom let him play outside as much as he wanted. He had a dog named Okie, a sling-shot, and an awesome treehouse his dad built. The tree was full of pink mangoes, jabbering parrots, and fat iguanas! When he was older, his family moved home to Oklahoma, and he began second grade. His favorite classes were Reading and History. He still got to spend a lot of time outdoors, and sometimes his uncles would take him hunting—with their falcons! His favorite tales were *Treasure Island*, *The Swiss Family Robinson*, *Old Yeller*, and *The Hobbit*.

After finishing 19 years(!) of school, Brandon went to work as an attorney. In 2001, a lovely lady agreed to marry Brandon. Now they have five great kids and live on the Oklahoma plains. Regarding Prince Martin, Brandon didn't even know he existed until he popped into his head one day! And when he had to go overseas for a long time in 2015, Brandon would tell his young son Prince Martin stories on the phone. In fact, the boy named some of the most important characters! Now Brandon wakes up real early every morning (when the house is unusually quiet) and writes about Prince Martin. His previous books in the Prince Martin Epic are *Prince Martin Wins His Sword* and *Prince Martin and the Thieves. Prince Martin and the Dragons* is his third book—and he's got more up his sleeve!

ABOUT THE ILLUSTRATOR

Jason Zimdars is an artist and designer who has always loved to draw. He grew up immersed in stories of heroes and magic like *The Lord of the Rings*, *Star Wars*, *The Dark Crystal*, and *E.T.* He always came home from the movies or the library to draw all the amazing characters and places he saw in his imagination.

When his friend, Brandon, told him about Prince Martin he knew he had to draw him and all his friends, too. *Prince Martin and the Dragons* is his third book. He can't wait to share more of Prince Martin's adventures with you!

Jason lives in Oklahoma with his teenage daughter and two dogs, who aren't nearly as brave as Sir Ray.

For More Information

www.princemartin.com
info@princemartin.com

Made in United States
Troutdale, OR
11/16/2024

24887687R00056